Ruby was built in 1934 by the Austin Motor Company in Longbridge, England. She's shiny, she's beautiful, *and* she could be yours.

Hidden in the pictures of this book are the six letters and numbers that appear on her license plate. Look very carefully to find the right combination—but beware, it's tricky! When you think you've found the correct letters and numbers, complete the entry form and mail it in. You can find details on the back flap of the book jacket.

Who knows?... *You* could win Ruby for yourself!

Good luck!

Ruby

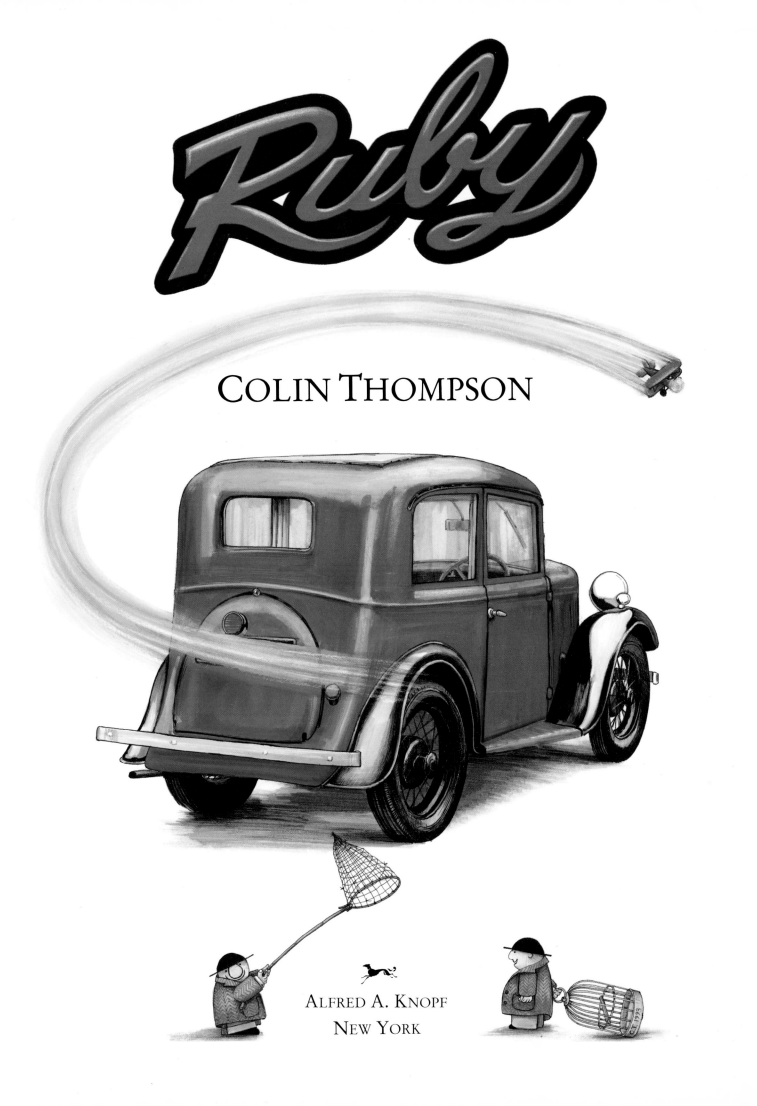

COLIN THOMPSON

ALFRED A. KNOPF

NEW YORK

For Heather
and for Roger,
who started it all

THIS IS A BORZOI BOOK
PUBLISHED BY ALFRED A. KNOPF, INC.

Copyright © 1994 by Colin Thompson

All rights reserved under International and Pan-American
Copyright Conventions. Published in the United States of
America by Alfred A. Knopf, Inc., New York, and simultaneously
in Canada by Random House of Canada Limited, Toronto.
Distributed by Random House, Inc., New York.

Library of Congress Cataloging-in-Publication Data

Thompson, Colin
Ruby / Colin Thompson
p.   cm.
Summary: The members of a miniature family come
to the rescue when young Kevin climbs aboard a car
and becomes trapped in a suitcase.
ISBN 0-679-86744-9 (trade)
[1. Size—Fiction. 2. Automobiles—Fiction. 3. Family life—
Fiction.]   I. Title.
PZ7.T371424Ru 1994 [E]—dc20 93-50924

Manufactured in Singapore
10 9 8 7 6 5 4 3 2 1

In the roots of a tree on the edge of a field lived a family of small, contented people. George and Mavis had lived there all their lives and so had their children, Kevin and Tracy. Only Uncle Austin had been in the outside world. Only he knew about its wonderful and terrible ways.

1934

The real Ruby was made in 1934 in Longbridge, England. The border throughout this book shows what could have happened to an Austin 7 between 1934 and today.

George and Mavis peered out from the hole at the bottom of the tree. In the soft green shadow beneath its wide branches was an old car, and beyond the car two people were sitting on the grass having a picnic.

"Look at all that food," said Mavis. "There's enough there to feed the five of us for a year."

"I'm going to get some," said Kevin, and he ran off toward the car. His little hat bobbed up out of the grass as he jumped up to see where he was going, and a few seconds later he was climbing up the wire spokes of the wheel. There was a large picnic basket on a rack at the back of the car, and Kevin made straight for it. He vanished behind the wheel, reappeared on the back bumper, then scrambled up the side of the basket and disappeared inside.

The afternoon sun began to slide below the tall hedge on the far side of the field. The sky changed from blue to gold, and rabbits peered out nervously from their beds. The people on the grass packed up their picnic and prepared to leave.

"Where's Kevin?" said Tracy. They all began to call, but there was no sign of him. By this time the woman was sitting in the car and the man was doing up the last strap on the basket. "We'll have to go after him," said George.

"But . . ." began Mavis.

"There's no time for *but*," said George, grabbing her hand and running toward the car. Tracy ran past them and was up on the back bumper before they reached the wheel. Uncle Austin came up behind, puffing and blowing like an old train.

"It'll end in tears," he muttered.

"Never mind all that," said George. "Just get up here before the wheels start moving."

As they scrambled up the car, the man turned the starting handle, and the engine began to sing.

The car went off across the field, moving softly through the grass. George looked back at the tree that had been the center of his whole world and felt a lump come to his throat. Mavis reached out and took his hand.

"We'll be all right," she said.

The car pulled out into the lane, sat quietly while the man shut the gate, and then set off toward the distant town. Behind the spare tire George and Mavis sat on an oily rag, too miserable to move. Uncle Austin lay back beside them and was soon fast asleep. Tracy sat on her mother's knee and fidgeted.

The lane became a road and the road became a highway. Mile after mile they traveled. The air was filled with new smells none of them had ever experienced before, violent smells from thundering trucks that drowned the real smells of summer. At last they left the highway. The car slowed down and turned into a small garage. The people got out, locked the garage doors, and left the family in silent darkness.

MAXIMUM LOAD 56 LBS
PRO PAT

"Is everyone all right?" asked George.

"Where's my Kevin?" said Mavis. "Come on, we've got to get that basket undone."

"It's gone," said Tracy. "The people took it."

Mavis was beside herself. "My poor little baby!" she cried. "I'll never see him again."

"I said it would end in tears," muttered Uncle Austin.

Behind them, inside the car, there was a faraway voice, like a ventriloquist's dummy shut inside a suitcase.

"That's Kevin!" said Tracy. "He's inside the car."

George gripped Mavis's hand. Mavis took Tracy's, and Tracy reached out for Uncle Austin. The four of them, their eyes now accustomed to the darkness, squeezed through a little hole behind the spare tire and found themselves inside the car. The moon was shining through the garage window, covering the soft red leather seat with blue light.

"Kevin," called Mavis. "Where are you?"

The voice was much louder now, and it was ahead of them. They crept to the front of the seat and looked down. There was a briefcase on the car floor, and Kevin's voice was inside it with the rest of him. He had fallen off the seat into the open case, and as he had landed, the lid had closed, locking him inside. George put his mouth to the edge of the lid and shouted, "Can you hear me, son? Are you okay?"

"Yes, Dad," said Kevin. "I've found a bag of potato chips."

"My poor baby," said Mavis. "He's so little."

"Don't worry," said George. "We'll soon have him out of there."

George and Uncle Austin pulled at the briefcase locks, but they wouldn't open. There were little windows next to each lock with numbers and letters inside them.

"That's a combination, that is," said Uncle Austin. "You need the right numbers and letters to open them."

"Oh, my poor Kevin!" cried Mavis. "He's going to suffocate."

"No, he's not," said Uncle Austin. "He's got enough air for hours."

"Hang on!" shouted George. "We'll soon have you out of there."

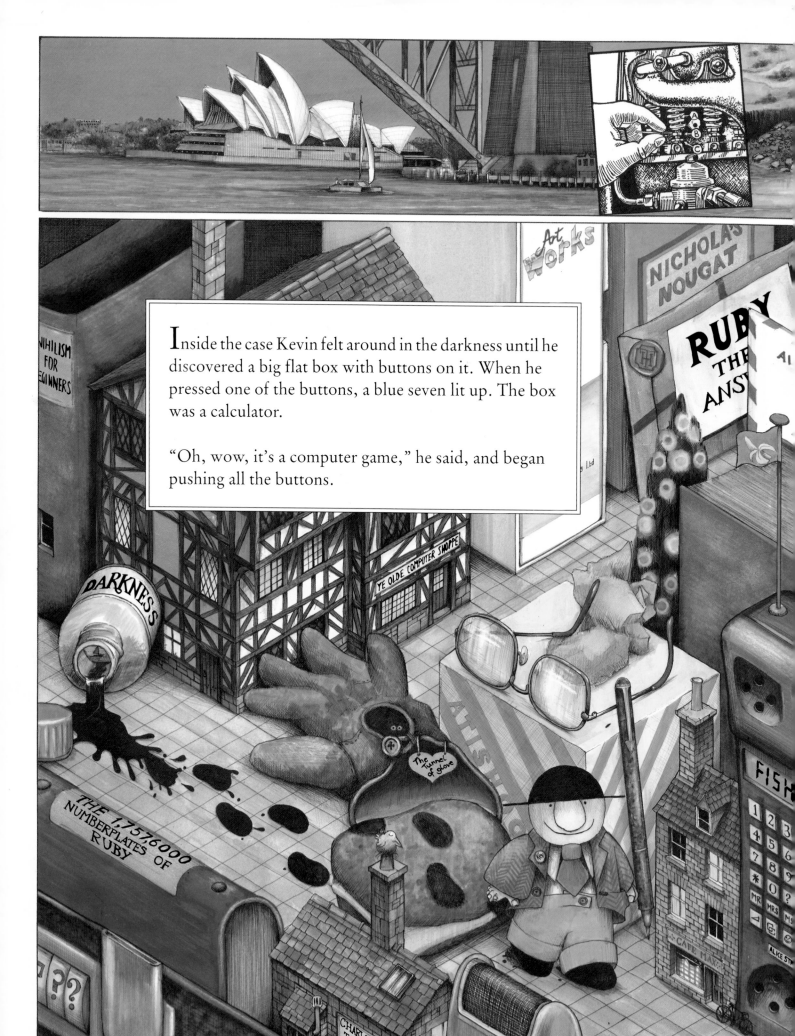

Inside the case Kevin felt around in the darkness until he discovered a big flat box with buttons on it. When he pressed one of the buttons, a blue seven lit up. The box was a calculator.

"Oh, wow, it's a computer game," he said, and began pushing all the buttons.

On the back seat there was a man's jacket. George climbed into the pockets and threw everything out.

"Maybe he's got the combination to the lock written down somewhere," he said as they sorted through it all. There were scraps of paper with all sorts of things written on them, but nothing that looked as if it might open the case.

"You don't write it down," said Uncle Austin. "You just keep it in your head."

"It must be written down *somewhere*," said George. "What if you forgot it?"

"One hundred and eighty!" shouted Kevin from inside the case.

There was a Filofax under the jacket, and while George and Mavis looked through the pages and called out all the numbers, Tracy sat on the floor trying them on the locks.

After an hour they had reached the last page in the Filofax and the case was still locked. They climbed up into the glove compartment, but there was nothing in it to help them.

George and Mavis got up onto the dashboard and looked out the windshield, through the garage window, and up at the stars. On the car floor Tracy scratched around under the seats looking for clues. The town was asleep now, with only the murmur of traffic on the highway and the faint snoring of Uncle Austin to disturb the quiet.

George put his arm around Mavis and tried to cheer her up by saying, "Your hat looks lovely in the moonlight, just like a new mushroom."

"Nine hundred and four!" shouted Kevin.

Suddenly there was a wet, snorting, coughing noise right beside them, and the ashtray seemed to explode. Mavis grabbed George, and George grabbed the window frame as a bald green head shot up through a cloud of cigarette ash.

"Hello," said the green head, "who are you?"

George and Mavis explained who they were and why they were there. Tracy climbed up beside them and blushed bright red because she thought he was the handsomest creature she had ever seen.

"Hello," she said shyly. "My name's Tracy."

"Virus," said the green creature, bowing low.

"Two thousand and forty!" shouted Kevin.

"You haven't got anything to eat, have you?" said Virus. "I haven't eaten for days."

"Why not?" asked Tracy.

"There's nothing left," said Virus. "I've even eaten the filters."

"Haven't you tried anything else?" asked Mavis. "A nice beetle or a slug perhaps?" Virus looked even greener. Tracy picked up a dead fly and said, "Go on, try it. These are my very favorite." And because Virus thought that Tracy was the most beautiful creature *he* had ever seen, he took a deep breath, closed his eyes, and put the fly in his mouth.

After a minute he said, "Is it an acquired taste?" But he swallowed it.

While Tracy searched for more flies, George and Mavis climbed down to the floor and squeezed past the brake pedal into the engine compartment. There were numbers everywhere, but George didn't think any of them would be the right one.

The night moved slowly on. By two o'clock the highway had fallen silent and the world lay crisp under a starlit sky. In the heart of the engine, George and Mavis were asleep, curled up on the dynamo. In the ashtray Tracy and Virus slept among the ash and flies' legs. On the back seat Uncle Austin snored, and in the briefcase Kevin fell asleep on top of the calculator.

When George and Mavis woke up, their backs were stiff and they were cold. They dropped down from the engine onto the garage floor and jumped up and down to get warm. A few minutes later Tracy and Virus appeared.

"Twenty three million!" shouted Kevin, and then the batteries went dead and he was left in total darkness.

Uncle Austin woke with a snort and said, "Has it ended in tears yet?" He stumbled out of the car, and as the others turned toward him, the first rays of the day's sun shone through the window onto the car's license plate.

"That's it!" cried George. "That's the number." And it was.

That afternoon they found a large tree at the bottom of the garden and had a long sleep.

Mavis said they should work out a plan to get home. The others agreed, but summer turned into autumn and autumn into winter, and all they wanted to do was hibernate.

"We'll go home next spring," said George, but everyone was fast asleep.